Read to Me

just one more book

written and illustrated by
Pamela A. Kopen, M.D.
with introduction by
Dan F. Kopen, M.D.

PADAKAMI PRESS
Forty Fort, PA

Read to Me! Just one more book?

Illustrations Copyright © 1991 by Pamela A. Kopen, M.D.
Text Copyright © 1991 by Pamela A. Kopen, M.D.

Published by Padakami Press,
a division of Padakami Enterprises,
23 Dana Street, Forty Fort, Pa. 18704

Illustrations by Pamela A. Kopen, M.D.

Drawings done in pen and ink, with water soluble colors.

Printed by Llewellyn & McKane, Inc.
Bound by Horowitz/Rae Book Manufacturers, Inc.

First Edition

Published in the United States of America
10 9 8 7 6 5 4 3 2 1

Library of Congress Catalog Card Number
91-60425

ISBN 0-962-89140-1

with love to James, Krystin, and Kaytlin
whose innocent and insatiable curiosity
inspired this book,
and with gratitude to their "Nana" and "Pop Pop"
whose experienced and patient guidance
has made it all possible — P.A.K.

Introduction

A love of children, an appreciation for shared reading, and the enjoyment of teddy bears combined to inspire this book.

As parents we share a desire to help direct the early education of our children. These early lessons will lay a foundation of abilities and attitudes for a lifetime of learning. We want that foundation to be intellectually strong and morally secure.

The importance of reading in our information age cannot be overstated. Effective communication skills are critical to all pursuits. In mankind's age-old search for truth and understanding we are critically dependent upon a foundation of literacy.

For our children, as for us, there are intervals when we are especially receptive to the acquisition of knowledge and the acceptance of ideas. This concept of the "teachable moment" has long been recognized by educators. Observing our own children, we have noted that the period before retiring to sleep seems to be a particularly good time for planting the seeds for future intellectual development. This interval of one-half to one hour serves as fertile soil in which knowledge and attitudes often take root and thrive.

Perhaps this is a period when a child's seemingly boundless physical energies have been depleted, but a reservoir of inquisitiveness exists. This presents us with an unusually good opportunity to focus our children's curiosity without the distractions of excess physical activity. Our shared thoughts and feelings seem more likely to leave lasting impressions on our children during these periods.

Adding significance to the sharing of time with our children is the concept of "psychologic time." Unlike chronologic, or everyday time, the passage of psychologic, or perceived time, accelerates as we age. The result is a perceived shortening of periods such as hours, days, and weeks as we grow older. For a child, an hour represents a much greater block of time than it does for an adult. The opportunity afforded by this differential in time perception is that an offering of an hour by a parent is received as a gift of much greater magnitude by a child.

Paraphrasing the words of our 19th century American poet, H. W. Longfellow, we invite you sometime in the quiet of the evening to take pause from your preoccupations and engage in your children's hour.

— D.F.K.

Read to Me

just one more book

the petition

Read to me! I want to learn
as much as I can know…

Of laughs,
and cries,
and butterflies,

Of wind,

and sun,

and snow

Of distant shores,

and dinosaurs,

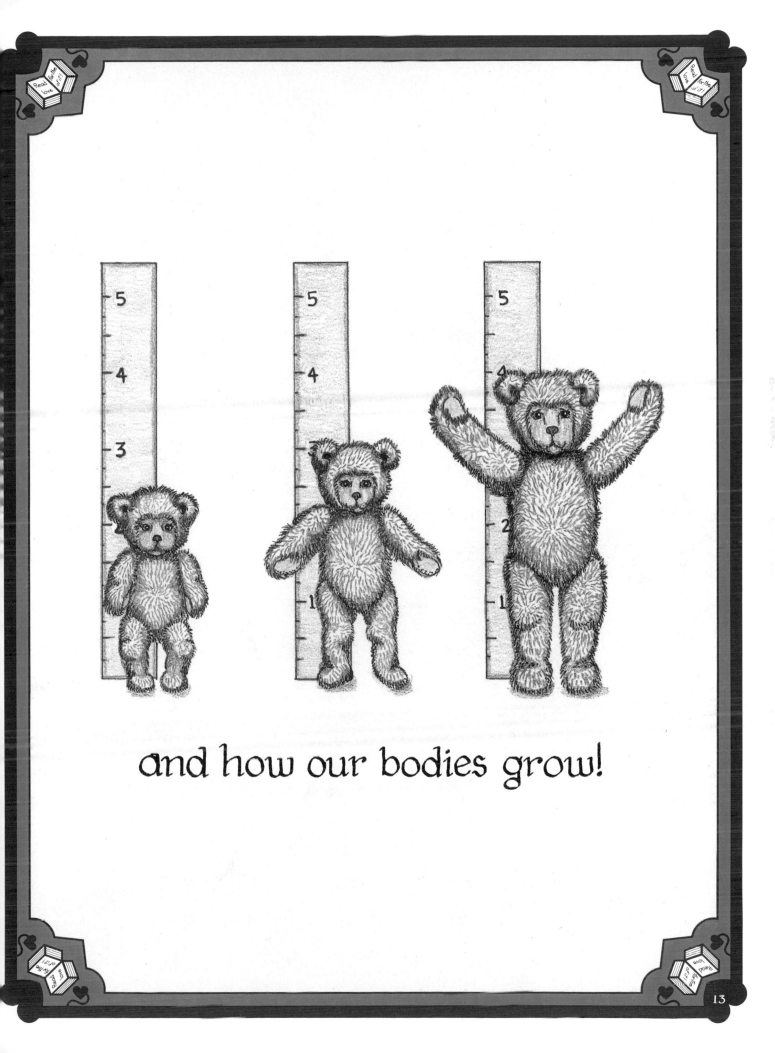

and how our bodies grow!

I want to hear again
about the clouds up in the skies,

To snuggle up right next to you,
to look into your eyes···

While asking all my questions—
all my "What"s ?
and "How"s ?
and "Why"s ?

Oh, read to me...
    just one more book?
And then I'll close my eyes.

I'll read to you,
my precious one,
with love, and with delight··

As shadows lengthen,
and the day
surrenders to the night..

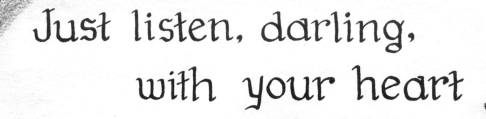

Just listen, darling,
with your heart

And let your thoughts
take flight!

But, be patient, my petitioner,

in case I just don't know

the answers to your questions

such as · · ·

"What makes breezes blow?"

"Why's the sun so warm and bright?"

"How do snowflakes grow?"

Together, sweetheart, let's embark,

We'll read of joys and woes.

We'll travel through the pages

as our understanding grows...

And even though each answer
may let other questions flow...

I'll read to you,
my precious one,
because I LOVE YOU SO!

Read to Me

just one more book

— The Petition —

Read to me! I want to learn as much as I can know . . .
   of laughs, and cries, and butterflies,
   of wind, and sun, and snow;
   of distant shores, and dinosaurs,
      and how our bodies grow!

I want to hear again about the clouds up in the skies . . .
   to snuggle up right next to you,
   to look into your eyes
      while asking all my questions —
      all my "What"s,
         and "How"s,
            and "Why"s.

Oh, read to me . . . just one more book?
   and then I'll close my eyes.

— The Response —

I'll read to you, my precious one,
   with love and with delight,
   as shadows lengthen, and the day
    surrenders to the night.

Just listen, darling, with your heart,
   and let your thoughts take flight!

But, be patient, my petitioner, in case I just don't know
   the answers to your questions, such as . . .
     "What makes breezes blow?" or . . .
     "Why's the sun so warm and bright?" or . . .
     "How do snowflakes grow?"

Together, sweetheart let's embark,
   We'll read of joys and woes.
   We'll travel through the pages
    as our understanding grows;
   And even though each answer
    may let other questions flow . . .

I'll read to you, my precious one,
   because I LOVE YOU SO!